BOOK OF FEAR

A SUSPENSEFUL SHORT HORROR STORY

I0623539

EERIE ACADIA
BOOK ONE

MARY BLACK ROSE
BLACK ROSE READS

BLACK ROSE MEDIA ARTS

Amazon
ISBN-13: 978-1-950211-59-3
D2D
ISBN-13: 978-1-950211-60-9

Published by Black Rose Media Arts LLC
Inquiries email – blackrose.media.arts@gmail.com

This is a work of fiction. Names, characters, businesses, places, events, locales, and incidents are either the products of the author's imagination or used in a fictitious manner. Any resemblance to actual persons, living or dead, or actual events is purely coincidental.

Welcome To Eerie Acadia!

In the tiny New England town of Acadia, Connecticut, strange and paranormal occurrences unfold more often than not. The town inhabitants are trapped in a vortex of both enchanted and cursed experiences, each with a unique tale to tell.

Welcome, to the strange little town where you will find creepy and charming stories alike! We hope you'll settle in with a cup of tea and stay awhile. Maybe you too, will never leave!

WHY ACADIA IS ENCHANTED...

The Origin Story!

Why do strange things always happen in Acadia?

SYNOPSIS: Nora knows that her aspirations to be a librarian are quaint and uninspiring, but she doesn't care. She likes knowing what to expect in life. It comes as a great surprise when her friend mentions the 'Restricted Section' hidden in the town library and she becomes downright obsessed to learn more. It's rumored that no soul has visited since a girl died from reading forbidden books, years ago. Now, Nora will stop at nothing to find out what's behind the door of the 'RESTRICTED SECTION!'

CHAPTER ONE

I'm unsure how old I was when I discovered the book. Probably about thirteen or fourteen. It left its mark, and I was forever changed after that.

In order to understand my story and why I did what I did, I have to back up and give you a bit of a personal history outline.

The summer of 1995 after 7th grade was magical. The best I'd ever had.

I walked along the street. School had just let out, and I had a head full of plans and schemes.

"What do you want to do tonight?" Maddy asked me.

"Movie-a-thon! Definitely need to get to the video store and rent all three 'Back To The

Future' movies. You get the videos and I'll make the popcorn."

"Sounds like a plan!" Maddy grinned.

We walked by Michelle's house quickly, hoping she wouldn't notice us. When the coast was clear, we went our separate ways, excited for the summer vacation to begin.

That summer was the best, but I guess life throws you some easy pitches sometimes, then it moves onto cruel curve balls that hit you right in the gut, leaving you doubled over in pain, panting and trying to catch your breath.

My best friend Maddy and I had been friends since the crib. Literally baby-buddies. Our mothers walked us in our strollers together. Growing up in houses that were side by side, we couldn't help but become friends or enemies. Luckily, we became friends, but that wasn't the case of our other neighbor.

Maddy and I were a united front against our enemy, Michelle. My house was in the middle of the two girls. If you found yourself walking up to my front door, Maddy lived on the left and Michelle on the right.

There was a time in preschool and kindergarten where the three of us played together at times, but it was always strained –

Michelle competing to be the leader and boss of both of us. I often found myself excluded for reasons I couldn't fathom. Perhaps this should have been foreshadowing, but it's not like you pay attention to that kind of shit when you're only a kid.

As we approached our tween years things began to change. Then the middle school years came into play and lines in the sand were no longer dim.

Michelle became the quintessential, popular, cheerleader, and well, Maddy and I were not.

Looking back, it's crazy how you can be BFF's with someone one week, and they can utterly become your worst nightmare the next. Michelle was that type of girl to Maddy and I. We dreaded PE class where she flaunted her backflips, walkovers, and splits.

Michelle had been in gymnastics since she was three, but she had no shame in belittling us for being unmatched in her athletic prowess. She wore it all like a badge of the highest honor that she could outdo most of her classmates. Her other cheerleading cronies followed her lead, showing off and shaming anyone who couldn't keep up.

Maddy and I matured slower than the other girls. While they were all wearing makeup and reading boyband magazines, Maddy and I still wanted to play in the treehouse.

So yeah, the magic of 7th grade summer slowly transitioned into 8th grade being tolerable.

When 8th grade started, I had no idea my life was about to plummet into a deep dark hole of chaos.

I was already disappointed beyond belief that Maddy was being shipped off to a summer camp so her parents could go on a season long cruise.

I was lost without my BFF. As long as I had Maddy, we could conquer the world. Even if that world consisted mostly of adults who just didn't understand, and hormone acne faced teens with their own agendas.

We wrote each other letters religiously the first few weeks. Then, they started to taper off. I'd barely gotten any by the time summer camp was winding down for her.

When she got back, I sensed immediately that she was changed, but I didn't want to believe it. She seemed distant and aloof. She seemed prettier and I was shocked and amazed. My naïve, stupid-self wouldn't realize what this meant until school started.

When Maddy went to camp, the girls in her bunk had befriended her – turned her into their project makeover. I got a feeling these girls were like Michelle, and they taught her how to change herself in a way that I never thought either of us capable of.

Whatever those girls did to Maddy in the two short months, it was beyond my comprehension. She went from shy and introverted to a shallow sort of extrovert. They taught her how to style her hair, makeup, and clothing. She was completely transformed, and I barely recognized her.

At first, she hung out with me, but that quickly shifted.

She could do pristine cartwheels and the splits, and she showed off her moves in gym class. Michelle and the others were impressed. It was just enough to land her a place on the junior squad when try outs came up two weeks after school started.

I think that marked the beginning of the end. The nail in the coffin of our friendship would come a little later.

She was never unkind to me, but it was clear she didn't want to hang out with me anymore either. She'd only make eye contact and wave at me if no one else was looking. It didn't take a lot for me to realize that I'd lost my best friend to the girls I loathed the most.

To say I was devastated was an understatement. Going to school was as tolerable as I could make it, as I navigated the complicated emotion of grief over losing my best friend. I was managing to survive until Michelle decided to make me the object of her bullying. She moved around from target to target. I suppose boredom induced her to change it up? Who knows.

About three weeks into school, and gym class found me at the center of her attention – and not in the limelight sort of way.

It began with light teasing about my hair, then my clothes, and so on.

I watched Maddy closely. Waiting for her to speak up on my behalf. I felt as if the earth had bottomed out and eaten me alive when I realized no rescue from my old friend would occur.

I managed to get through class and when the bell rang, I ran to the bathroom stall, and cried my eyes out. I left school and didn't care that I'd just cut class for the first time in my life. I'd tell my mother I was sick and throwing up. It wasn't a lie. I was that upset.

CHAPTER TWO

I suppose I could say luckily Michelle moved on, and I managed to steer clear of her machinations. However, the damage was done, and I was devastated and damaged in a way I couldn't define.

I stumbled through each day feeling like it was simply a game of going through the motions. I did just enough to get by. I was depressed and hated my life.

My parents, having raised two boys, my older brothers ahead of me, chalked it up to teen angst. When I tried to talk to Mom about it, she brushed me off saying that it was a fleeting time in my life. Everything would change before I knew it and I'd probably have new friends within the week. I was pretty sure that wasn't the case, but I just nodded and sulked off.

I guess I was feeling nostalgic, so I stumbled into the woods behind our house. I found myself crunching through the new Autumn leaves and was headed on autopilot towards Maddy and I's old treehouse in the woods.

Her Dad had helped us build it when we were in third grade and we'd played so many games, so many tea parties, so many camp outs there...

I wiped the tears from my eyes as I found myself staring up at the crooked structure. I didn't think I'd go up. No, that would be torturing myself beyond reason.

I took one last look at it and kept going on the game path that was just beyond that big tree. I wasn't sure where I was going. I just knew I didn't want to be home.

I didn't see it at first. I tripped over something protruding out from the leaves along side of the game trail.

I looked down and was shocked to see what looked like the corner of a large book.

I stooped down and brushed the leaves away to find that it was a book. It was a huge, leather book, with faded gold lettering that had letters in a language I couldn't understand. It seemed antique. It was a tome like you might see open on the pulpit of some gothic church stand.

I picked it up and it felt heavier than I would have thought. It was bigger and thicker than your average book.

I was still crouched down and placed it on the edge of my lap as I balanced, and looked around for the source of who might have dropped this book. Then I remembered it being buried in the leaves and thought it must have been there for a few days at the very least.

I stood up and clutched it to my chest.

A strange feeling overcame me. I felt guilty standing there with this book, as if I shouldn't be caught with it. I wanted to explore the pages within. I felt a compulsion that I needed to read this book. My eyes darted around looking for anyone who might see me with it, but there was no one. I was alone.

I noticed that the sun was setting. It was getting dark, and the woods had become eerily and unnaturally quiet.

I took off running back to my house. I didn't stop. I just ran, with this foreboding feeling, ever mounting, that something was chasing me. That it was going to overtake me and reclaim the book. When I crossed the threshold of the forest tree line in my backyard, I was breathless, and terrified for no rational reason.

I quickly looked over my shoulder and slowed my pace as I realized there was no one there.

I laughed uneasily at my stupid imagination getting the better of me.

And yet, there was something that I couldn't quite put a finger on. I scurried inside and locked the door. I would be home alone for the next two hours with mom at her book club, dad working late, and my brothers out doing whatever they did on a random day.

I sat down on my bed and released the book. It fell into the quilt with a soft 'thud' sound. I sat cross legged on my bed and lightly touched the cover. I was shocked that the letters seemed less faded. I felt as though I was going crazy. Maybe a trick of the light. That had to be it.

I opened the book and the first page held the same foreign words as the cover reading phonetically, "Liber Timoris."

I didn't know what language that was.

My father was very keen on all the latest and greatest technology and I took the book into the family den where our computer was. I booted it up and waited impatiently for the beeps and boops of the dial up to connect to the Internet.

Dad had just been showing us this fairly new thing we could use on the Internet called WebCrawler. I thought I'd give it a try. He'd been trying to get me to use it for research papers and such, but my school wasn't keen on me citing that kind of research yet. They still wanted me to use the Encyclopedia Britannica's and the Dewey Decimal system at the library to find my research books.

I simply typed in 'liber timoris' and found a list of possible sources. The third one down looked promising, so I clicked on it.

The article read:

"Liber Timoris" – "The Book of Fear" – is an urban legend that has circulated for decades amongst psychic mediums and occultists. The book is said to have been

created by a powerful cult or coven of wealthy individuals that have gone by the name "Dator Lucis Slausis."

The book is rumored that the owner must abide by the pact they make with the spirit of the book.

The pact being that they must survive one night – sundown to sunrise – of their worst fears. By the light of dawn, if they have not died, they speak their wish and it will be granted.

The book will then find a new owner. This book has become a dark fairy tale of sorts in the world of urban legends amongst dark mystics and fortune tellers, as no one has ever seen the book and perhaps if they have, lived to tell about it. It is regarded as local lore and legend; nothing more.

I read over the short description a few times, thinking, 'pact?' How does one make a pact with a book?

I glanced down at the book sitting at the edge of the computer desk, and nearly stumbled out of my chair. The cover was no longer written in some foreign language. It was written in English, and I could read the shiny gold embossing perfectly. It now said, "The Book of Fear."

My breathing was ragged, and I didn't know what to do. I just stared at the cover. Some niggling part of my brain thought that the letters now looked newly embossed. The leather no longer looked worn and old. It was as if the book had been crafted a mere few hours ago.

I didn't know what to do. Then the whispering started. It was so low at first, I thought the computer fans were to blame. Then it was all around me and there was no mistaking that it was not coming from the computer at all.

The whispers were like that of many people trying to talk to me at once – insistent and urgent, but I couldn't make out what they were saying. I was terrified, and I ran to my room, my hands clasped over my ears, screaming, "Leave me alone!"

I slammed my door shut and all at once the whispering stopped. I was in tears, and I slumped down on my bed. There was something that broke in me then. The entire summer spent alone and isolated, the excitement of the new school year with Maddy only to be betrayed in the worst way possible, and now this.

I pulled at my hair and screamed a shrill primal scream, and then I broke down crying. Great heavy, body wracking sobs – the culmination of anguish pent up for weeks and months, coming to a head.

When I'd finally cried out the last of my tears, I realized I had to do something about that book in the family office. I didn't want anything to do with this book. I had to take it back to the forest.

And yet, what if it was true? What if I could face a night of my fears to grant me one single wish? I already knew what I'd wish for. I wanted my friend back. I wanted things to go back to the way they were before.

However, even if this book held the power to do that, it meant I'd have to face all of my fears in one night. I wasn't brave or strong. There's no way I'd last. And even the article on the World Wide Web had said that no one had probably lived to tell the tale, hence why the book was merely an urban legend.

Yet, here I had such a book in my possession that might very well be THE Book of Fear. I mulled over the possibilities for a long time but ultimately decided that the book was bad news.

I resolved right then and there that I didn't want to explore this strange book. It felt off, and the things I'd already experienced – the strange phenomenon of the book changing and the whispers, was terrifying enough. If it could do that, I didn't want to see what other powers it had to induce greater fear in me.

I stood up, my legs were trembling. I could barely force myself to walk back to the family den. There was the book, sitting on the desk, just as I had left it. I wasn't expecting that. I was certain I'd come back and there would be something amiss, yet there wasn't.

I tentatively picked it up and quickly made my way to the kitchen and then out to the garage. I put it on a shelf. Covered it with one of dad's automotive, cleaning towels, and went back inside.

I heaved out a sigh of relief. First thing tomorrow I would take the book back to the woods. I was lucky that the following day was Saturday.

Chapter Three

I lay in bed for a long time before sleep took me. I couldn't stop thinking about it. Part of me still wanted to entertain the idea of what if. But then I ran through all my fears and wondered how they would manifest. The article said I could die. I didn't think that dying for one wish would be worth it.

And yet, wouldn't it be? Wouldn't it be worth it to risk everything to have my friend back? I wanted that but didn't think I could brave through every single fear I held.

I thought of spiders, and deep waters. I thought of Friday the 13th and how Freddy Kruger was the worst horror movie icon I'd ever watched on VHS, and I'd not been able to sleep well for weeks after.

I thought of Mr. Elden who always gave me the creeps and how much I hated shop class with him. Then, I thought of my Great Aunt Nellie who'd I'd met only a few times when I was three and the last time we met, how she'd turned into a living nightmare of a monster.

And after I'd exhausted my long, long, long list of fears, my thoughts circled back to Michelle. I hated myself for it. I was afraid of her. I hated her and I hated how she made me feel both little and afraid of her.

I wasn't sure what I was afraid of when it came to her, but I knew I was. And I considered that maybe I could face my other fears, but with Michelle, I wasn't sure I could. The source of my fear was so irrational, I couldn't play out any scenarios of how I would handle her. Because of this, I couldn't conceive how I would react. There was no reference point for me to form a plan.

Eventually, I fell asleep. I woke up with the light of dawn just peeking through my thin blue gossamer curtains. I had been on my side, and I tried to roll over on my back and stretch my legs out but there was someone or something on the bed preventing me from doing this.

I sat up, terrified to see that damn book right on the bed. It was in the same exact place I'd thrown it down the day before.

I whimpered and drew the covers up around me. Then the whispering started again. It was soft and grew ever steadily louder and louder. I could make out the words this time – a terrible chant of two words – "Open me, open me, open me…"

Despite my resolve to not go through with it, I found my hand reaching for the book, and pulling back the cover. As soon as I turned back the front cover to reveal the first page, the chanting suddenly ceased. The quiet that replaced the whispers was just as unnerving.

I stared down at the book and was terrified to see that the first page was no longer a title page as it was the day before. It was now, a letter addressed to me, by name.

Dear Susan,
You have claimed this book as yours, when you brought it home from its resting place in the woods. As such we are now bound to each other by a pact of living, breathing, magick.

You must fulfill the pact or be cursed to endure the voices of our chorus forever echoing in your mind until the pact is fulfilled.

Tonight, you must face your fears, and overcome them, every one. If you succeed, you will be granted one wish.
If you fail, we claim your soul and you are forever bound to the Life of The Book of Fear.

"No, no, no, no!" I breathed out. "I didn't want this. I didn't enter into a pact!"

I read the letter over and over again, but somewhere deep in my soul, I knew that it was true. When I'd touched the book and held it to my chest, it had already claimed me as its next victim. I wasn't running from something in the woods. I was running from the negative vibes that were right there against my chest.

This didn't seem fair. I felt I'd been tricked. If I'd known that merely touching the book, picking it up and bringing it home was enough to enter into the pact, I would have left it alone.

I picked the book up and dropped it on my desk. I thumbed through all the remaining pages, but they were blank. No, not blank, but the writing was so faded it was barely legible.

I strained to make out the words, but it was very difficult to read. I opened my curtains and went to the book. I could just barely make out in faded bluish ink, the names of people. Name after name after name of hundreds, if not thousands of names.

Fear seized my chest, and I began to hyperventilate. Were these the names of people whom the book claimed their lives? I couldn't help but think they were.

I slammed the book shut, trying to think of how to get out of this situation. I picked up the book, ran to the backyard, and threw the book into the fire pit. I went back to the garage, and grabbed dad's lighter fluid, and a box of matches.

I stood over the campfire pit, doused the book in fluid, lit a match and didn't even hesitate as I watched the fluid ignite in a huge plume of fire and smoke. I watched the fluid burn off, and to my dismay the book wouldn't catch. The flames licked at it and did absolutely nothing. When the fire died down the book was intact. I reached out to touch it and was not shocked when it was cool to the touch.

Tears welled up in my eyes. It would do no good to put the book back in the forest. Of course, it was naïve to think a magic book could just be destroyed with mere lighter fluid. It would not be destroyed so easily. It would seem I would have to face my fears.

I took the book back to my room and sat it on the edge of my desk. I looked over every page, and there was nothing in it that would prepare me for the night that lay ahead.

I spent the entire day writing in a notebook, every fear I could think of that I currently had or previously held. Then I wrote down all the ways they might manifest and how I would beat them. I was able to make a decent plan with most all of them, save the one that eluded me most. It was in the details that escaped my abilities to plan, that made my fears around this fear multiply even more.

The hours of the day passed more quickly than I could have imagined, and before I knew it, sundown was fast approaching.

Chapter Four

I sat on my bed watching the last rays of the sun dip below the tree line. I knew what was coming next. And yet, I also had no idea what to expect. I was shaking beyond control.

My eyes were randomly focused on the pattern of my quilt. I noticed a small thread that seemed to be moving. Why was that thread moving? It was dancing like a little snake.

I willed my body to stop shaking. It took all my effort, but the vibrations of my body were not causing this thread to wiggle as I had hoped.

Dread filled me, and I watched in horror as the thread began to push itself through an ever-growing hole. It was birthing itself through the bedding of my quilt. The thread became stiff and changed color. Then there were two limbs, then four, pushing themselves through, like a terrible birth canal.

An enormous spider, bigger than my cat, squeezed itself through the hole and then paused. It's hundreds of eyes locked on mine, as if seizing up its prey.

For a moment I was paralyzed. I had not imagined my arachnophobia to manifest in the form of a giant spider. I had imagined being overtaken by many spiders. Perhaps hundreds of them, and I would run to my shower and wash them all down the drain.

This was not at all what I had expected, and I had no plan of counterattack.

I whimpered as the archaic creature crawled slowly towards me. Stalking me. I couldn't move. I was frozen in terror.

Then suddenly it lunged at my face. Instinctively I swatted it away with much more force than I thought I was capable of. Its body hit the wall with a thud. I scrambled off the bed, keeping my eyes on it. It took a moment to untangle its limbs and right itself. Then it scurried under my bed across the room.

I waited, but the creature did not emerge. I slowly made my way to my desk and opened the drawer, continuing to keep my eyes on the bed as much as possible, I removed my pair of crafting scissors. They were old, all metal, given to me by my grandmother. The point was deadly sharp, and I held them in my hand like a knife.

I moved ever closer to the bed, just as my hand was about to lift the bed skirt, I heard a scuttling sound above me. I looked up just in time to see the creature falling down on my face.

It landed on my face and wrapped its legs around me, pulling me into its sharp incisors. I scrambled to tear its legs from its body, but they were not delicate like an ordinary house spider. I blindly stabbed at its body, and it screeched an ungodly cry of anguish.

I scrambled back and knew I only had moments to counterattack. I lunged forward and drove the scissors into its abdomen all the way to the hilt of the scissors. A putrid liquid exploded from its body, but there was no time to wipe it away from my eyes. I blinked hard, hoping it was not acidic, and twisted the scissors hard. The creature screamed in agony and then went limp.

My shoulders went lax, and I heaved a sigh of relief.

However, there would be little time to relax. The next fear was already manifesting.

The carpet felt wet. The spider's body dematerialized and floated away from me like ash on a breeze.

I touched my face and the gore from the dead spider was gone.

I had very little time to act as I realized the room was filling up with water. It was like an unseen pipe had burst and was saturating my carpet with ice cold water. I ran to the door to escape but of course it was locked. I pounded on it, but of course no one came. I took a chair to the window and tried to break it, but it wouldn't budge.

The water was pouring in now, and the items from my desk and nightstand began to float in the water. I didn't understand what was happening. All I could do was tread as the water rose higher and higher.

I was panicking. In only a moment I would be out of space to keep my head above water. I lifted my head back. My face flush with my bedroom ceiling. The water continued to rise, and then it overtook me. It covered my head entirely.

The streetlight from outside illuminating my room went out and I was plunged into darkness. I flailed, kicking hard to the surface, trying to break through. Just when I could hold my breath no longer, I broke the surface. I treaded water for a moment and felt the sweet relief of oxygen fill my lungs.

My triumph would only last a moment, as I looked around realizing I was alone in a vast, dark ocean that went on for as far as the eye could see. The waters were frigid, the sky was dark. Clouds covered most of the stars and moon. The waters were inky black. I was exhausted and yet, this was only the second fear to manifest.

I allowed myself a moment to rest and think. I laid back in the water and floated. I tried to calm my breathing.

I had no idea how to overcome this fear. The water was so cold, and my limbs were starting to lock up. I didn't know how cold the water was, but I knew that if it was cold enough, hypothermia could set in.

I suspected I didn't have much time. I tried to think about what the letter in 'The Book of Fear' had said. It said I had to face my fears and overcome them.

I was facing my fear of deep water right now but overcome it? How do I do that? I can't kill the ocean like I did the spider. I thought hard and it suddenly occurred to me that I had to move towards the fear. I couldn't always kill it. In this situation I had to move into the fear.

How does one do that?

My heart sank as I realized what I had to do. I began to hyperventilate. It was a crazy counterintuitive idea, but it was the only one I had. It had to work!

No, no, no, I didn't want to do this. But what other choice did I have? I knew there was no boat that would come along and rescue me. I had to try this, or I would die.

I realized, with an unusual calmness setting in, that I could either die trying to overcome my fear, or literally let my fear overtake me and die.

I didn't want to die at all, so I resolved to take my chances with the slightly better odds.

I huffed great deep breaths, filling my lungs with oxygen, then inhaled as deeply as I could, and dove down. Moving like a frog, I kicked my legs and pushed the water away from me. I wasn't sure what I was swimming towards, but I had to keep swimming down, deeper and deeper. I kept my eyes open, and all I could see was expansive darkness. A darkness that enveloped me entirely.

I continued on down, down, down, kicking and pushing the water back, and back. My lungs were burning. I didn't think I could hold my breath any longer. I wasn't going to make it, but I was going to try.

I couldn't do it. I couldn't hold my breath any longer and just as I inhaled, expecting water to fill my lungs, light burst forth, blinding me, and sweet oxygen filled my lungs.

CHAPTER FIVE

I panted and spit water out of my mouth. I crawled along not sure where I was going. I tumbled onto my back looking up at a white ceiling. It was dark and the ceiling tiles looked like I wasn't at home but rather a business or government building.

After my breathing steadied, I managed to pull myself up and looked ahead seeing the longest hallway that I'd ever seen. It stretched on for miles. The florescent lights overhead, casting an eerie and disturbing yellow glow, flickered.

I felt the presence of someone behind me and I turned around to see the outline of none other than Freddy Krueger himself. His long claw like hands elongated. The outline of that infamous hat.

I scrambled up and began to run. I felt as if my limbs were stuck in molasses. I couldn't move as quickly as I knew I should be able to. It was as if I was stuck in a real time horror movie. A bad dream of my own, within a movie that ironically starred me.

Terror gripped me, choked and squeezed my chest as I saw the visage of the movie monster move closer. Slowly at first and then more quickly.

Instinctively, I ran faster. I realized there were doors lining the hallway, and I stopped only for a few short moments to try them. Of course, they were all locked. I gave up on escaping through the doors and kept running.

At some point the lighting shifted from yellow to red. I ran until my legs ached and my lungs felt as if they were going to give out again. I slowed just enough to look behind me and realized he was gone. He wasn't there.

I wanted to believe that I'd conquered this fear, but some sinister premonition told me that was not the case. I stopped long enough to catch my breath, bending over at the waist, panting heavily.

"Hello, Susan."

I jerked upright and saw the pocked face of Freddy only inches from mine. He was wearing a frightening grin. I was about to turn and run, but before I could, his arm came down across my chest slashing me.

I looked down, shocked at the three huge gashes across my chest, now pouring blood from the wounds.

Up until now, I supposed all of this to be in my mind, but this was real. I was bleeding all over my clothes and the dingy brown carpet. I could feel the blood hemorrhaging from my gashes quickly, causing me to go into shock. I needed to move and yet I couldn't will myself to.

This was too much. I couldn't do this. No wonder there were so many names in the book.

"That's right, Susan," Freddy said. "You're a loser. You've always been last. You always lose. And tonight, I will claim your soul."

Something about his taunting caused me to bristle. I had two older brothers who'd spent my entire childhood calling me 'loser' and it triggered something fierce in me.

I stood upright, looked Freddy Krueger in the face, and screamed, the loudest, most primal scream I'd ever let out in my entire life.

I was shocked that Krueger looked surprised as well. Suddenly, I felt like an animal trapped in a cage and I was going to fight to my last drop of blood if need be. I lunged at Freddy and clawed and scraped at his face. I spit and kicked with wild abandon and uncontrolled rage. I found myself ripping at his necrotic flesh and torn clothes. Part of him began to break off, and I realized it was working.

I doubled my efforts and kept ripping and tearing at him.

Then just as quickly as he'd appeared, his visage and the ominous hallway were gone replaced by a surrounding that was familiar but not quite distinct yet.

It was dark and the lights were off. There were tables and large objects covered with cloth tarps. It smelled of saw dust. And suddenly I knew where I was. It was shop class and I knew what fear I'd be facing next; Mr. Elden my sixth-grade shop teacher.

All the girls hated him and at the end of sixth grade year he'd been fired and charged with assault of a minor. One of the girls in the school had come forward to accuse him of molesting her.

I'd always been afraid to go into his office alone. He'd stand too close and touch my shoulder in a way that felt inappropriate but how could I explain that to anyone? I was both shocked and not when Sara had come forward with her accusations. I knew she wasn't lying, but the school had been divided on the matter. It became so difficult for her, her family ended up moving out of state entirely so she could go to another school and start anew.

I stopped, suddenly feeling someone's hot breath on my neck. I was about to turn, but heard the sound of my teachers' voice as he trailed a finger down my neck.

I recoiled in horror as I stepped back. He always had this way of making me feel small and powerless. I hated it. I hated him. I hated his voice, his smell, everything about him.

"You should stop trying to run from me, Susan. You know you brought this on yourself. Why else would you come to my office after class to discuss your grade?"

"Because I actually needed to talk about my grade, Mr. Elden. It was unfair."

"Unfair. You had sloppy line work in your divots on the woodwork, and you know it." He pouted like an immature child, and it sent a chill up my spine.

"I— I—" Stammered to get my words out. I felt as if he was always one step ahead of me in what to say. I could never explain myself properly. I knew the grade was unfair.

Suddenly, I knew he'd given me that grade unfairly to get me into his office. That's what he did to all the girls. The ones who came to complain were the ones he preyed on.

Somehow, instinctively, I'd known this. I got out before he could do any further damage. But the whole experience left me feeling more afraid of him for reasons I could never define, until the situation with Sara came to light.

He advanced forward and said in a cajoling tone, "You know you want me, so stop fightin' it and come here."

The last part of his tone was commanding. At first my knee jerk reaction was to obey. The years of societal conditioning to listen to authority without question.

I found myself moving forward and he said in low sinister tone, "That's right. Come closer now."

I panicked then. I knew what he would do to me if he got his hands on me. I knew I'd suffer the same fate as poor Sara.

"No!" I shouted at him. My eyes darted around the large shop room for a path of escape, and I began to run. I could hear his heavy work boots thumping down as he pursued me. I looked around for anything I could use as a weapon and my eyes saw the wall at the very back.

It would mean I'd be trapped and have no choice. I looked around again. If I went the other way, there was a door.

I made a split-second decision. I knew from the past fears that running would do no good. I ran with all my strength to the back wall and removed the hammer from the peg. I turned to brace myself and Mr. Elden's tall lanky form strode towards me.

"Stupid little girl. You think you can overpower me?" He laughed.

I didn't respond. Just waited for him. After a long moment of staring at each other he jolted forward like a viper snapping at its prey. I was ready.

I lifted my arm up and brought the hammer straight into his forehead. Blood poured from his wound.

His expression was angry then.

"You think this will fucking stop me!" He roared. He removed the hammer as easily as one might pluck a bee stinger from their skin.

I ran again. The school workshop was easily three, four, five times the floor space it normally was. I wove through the quickly forming maze of tables and shop machinery that seemed to be forming a labyrinth of epic proportions.

I ran, trying to think what I might do next to face this fear. I didn't know what to do. No matter where I turned, he was right on my heels, only a step behind. I glanced over my shoulder and saw that his stature had doubled. All the features I hated about him, and there were so many, had become more grotesque.

His bulbous eyes were bulging even more so causing the blood vessels to burst with each obscenity he spewed at me. Blood still continued to pour from his wound. So much I could smell the coppery scent of it mixed with his nauseating cologne that I hated so much. I could feel his warm spittle falling on me like toxic rain. His boots stomped along, and I felt smaller and smaller as I continued to run. Twisted this way and that, moving haphazardly without purpose through the maze, with the monster of a man close on my heels.

I had to think. How to defeat my fear of him. My fear was because he made me feel small. I needed to get big; bigger than him.

Just as this thought had entered my mind, I saw a tree over the hedge. The shop class long gone replaced by a hedge maze. If I could make it to the tree, maybe I could climb it, get above him. And then what? I wasn't sure, but I had to make it to the tree.

Pure adrenaline propelled me down the corridors of hedges. I kept the top of the large oak tree in sight. I rounded a corner that opened up into the courtyard with the large tree in the center. I made for the tree and without looking back began to climb the large branches. I was not out of my element here and had no fear of heights. Maddy and I had climbed many trees just like this throughout my entire childhood.

When I made my way to the top, Mr. Elden who was a giant now, stood eye to eye with me.

I broke off a branch, wielding it like a sword as he came closer. He moved as if he was going to pluck me up by my shirt collar. Before he could, I jabbed him in one eye. He retracted his hand and slapped it over his eye.

"Little bitch!" He screamed.

He roared obscenities of rage at me and made to try again. I jammed the stick into his other eye. Blood poured from both orifices as well as the head wound.

"I am not small," I screamed at him.

Then an idea struck me, that if this magical landscape could shift and change, and I was interwoven into it, perhaps I could too.

I continued to scream, "I'm twice the human being you'll ever be!"

I felt myself growing and growing. The tree became small; as did Elden. I watched as my limbs and torso grew until I was so enormous, I could see the entire layout of the maze. It looked little more than a puzzle in one of my elementary school coloring books.

I stared down at Mr. Elden, and I knew what I would do next. Without hesitation, I lifted my foot, and like an ant, I squashed him beneath the sole of my shoe. I heard the satisfying crunch of his tiny bones crumble.

I exhaled a sigh of relief. The maze faded away. I shrunk back to normal size, and for a moment there was nothing. Just white for as far as the eye could see.

Then I blinked, and a scene from my past began to materialize. I heard the voice of someone I'd not heard in over ten years.

"Susan, where are you? Come here and let me see you, child?" The old voice crooned.

I got up from sitting on the floor and realized my body was shorter and smaller. I was a toddler again, and my mother was suddenly picking me up and taking me to my Great Aunt Nellie. I had this strange sensation of being myself as I was now, and yet also my smaller toddler self. A mixture of thoughts and how they were processed was also muddled between these two selves.

I fought through the mental fog and sheer blind primal fear coursing through me that I did not want to go near my aunt.

Something is wrong with her. My baby brain knew that. Then my adolescent brain processed that she had cancer. I learned this later in life, but at the time I was only three. I didn't understand why she looked, sounded, and smelled different. It was terrible. She was a woman who'd read me books and played dolls with me. Then they told me she was sick.

I was forced to say goodbye to her as she lay dying on her deathbed and now, here I was reliving one of the worst memories of my life.

I clutched at my mother's neck feeling a mixture of both confusion and understanding. I looked at Aunt Nellie, her shrunken emaciated form, her bald head with loose tendrils of hair sticking out, her breath rancid and they moved me ever closer to her.

She reached out a hand and I would not take it. My mother's tone both anguished and annoyed, "You need to say goodbye, Susan. Nellie is going away, and you won't ever see her again."

"No!" I screamed.

I could hear Aunt Nellie's raspy voice choking out, "It's okay, Linda, just let her be."

My mother insisting, "She's old enough to say her goodbyes, Nellie."

"No! No! No" I heard myself screaming.

The older part of me willed myself against the primal fear instincts of my toddler self to look at Nellie and what I saw was much worse than I remember.

Her skin was sloughing off, and she was coaxing me now as well. "Just one little kiss goodbye, Susan. Right here on my cheek. Say goodbye, now, to your poor ole' dying auntie…" She slowly moved her hand to point at her cheek and it was so thin and boney it could barely be construed as a human hand.

The stench of her breath as I was forced ever closer to her. The smell of decay and death filled my nostrils, and I thought I would be sick.

I could still feel my toddler self, resisting – fighting to get away, and screaming, "No! No! Get away from me!"

I tried to think outside of all the commotion, and again it became very clear what I needed to do.

I faced Nellie and reached out my small hand. I could see the fat chubby fingers touch down into her boney palm. I closed my eyes and kissed her on the cheek.

Instantly, my eyes flew open, and I saw her in her perfect form. She was healthy again, and she simply said, "I'm sorry, Susan." Her smile was very sad as she dissipated and I found myself standing in my room, alone in the dark.

CHAPTER SIX

I wanted to believe it was over, but I knew it wasn't. I knew that it was far from over. The night sky outside my bedroom window spoke volumes. I held my breath and waited.

I knew that it was the calm before the biggest storm I'd face tonight. It was time to face Michelle. Why was this harder than a giant spider, deep dark waters, an imaginary movie icon, a pedophile teacher, and my dying aunt?

I waited and nothing seemed to be happening. I wasn't sure what to do. I sat down on my bed and a glimmer of light beneath my bedroom door caught my eye. I heard the faintest noise that sounded like someone was watching TV in the living room.

I knew this was it. I didn't know what to expect as everything had taken place in the proverbial confines of my own room. Now I had to leave my room and venture out?

As soon as I turned the doorknob and swung the door open, I was met with a blast of loud music as if I'd just walked into a club. Furthermore, the hallway was not my house. It was someone else's.

I tentatively looked down the hallway. Teenagers from my school, faces I recognized were standing in the hallway in small groups. Some guys and girls were paired off kissing and making out. Some were just standing around talking, holding red cups.

There was shrill laughter, music pumping, lights strobing. In some ways the house seemed familiar and then it hit me. I was at Michelle's house and there was a party going on. I was horrified to look down and see I was dressed in my pajamas. I'd not changed my clothes from the night before when all of this BS had started.

If I was quick, I could sneak into the kitchen, out the back, and make it back to my house without being seen.

I made my way through the house, garnering strange looks from my classmates. I didn't care so long as I got out of there as quickly as possible.

Just as I was about to turn the knob on the backdoor, I heard a familiar voice call my name. "Susan, is that you?"

Maddy.

"Hey," I turned around. "I was just leaving," I tried again to get the hell out of there before things got ugly, and I knew it would. I just didn't know how.

"I didn't think you'd come. I mean everyone at school was invited to Michelle's birthd—" She stopped short and asked, "Why are you wearing your pajamas?"

"Uh, yeah. I thought it was a pajama party." I scratched the back of my neck nervously. "I need to go."

I turned again, but at that exact moment I heard Michelle's condescending tone, "Oh — My — God! What the hell are you wearing, Susan?" She laughed and all my other classmates that were flocked around her joined in.

"I was just leaving. Sorry, I got the details wrong," I mumbled.

"I know I said everyone was invited, but you are so stupid that you didn't realize that was just a formality to appease my parents. You weren't invited, but since you're here, you might as well stay."

She sauntered over and draped her arm around my shoulders as if we were old chums. I cringed.

"Take me back to the spiders and Elden. I can obviously handle that. I can't do this," I thought to myself.

I should have protested. Turned and left. But for some reason when Michelle interacted with me, it's like my brain shut down. I went non-verbal, catatonic. It was no different in real life or a magical world created by a cursed book.

Then in a soft tone, Michelle leaned in and whispered, "Besides, the party was boring. I'm sure now that you're here, we can find a way to liven things up."

She hooked her arm in mine and drug me against my will into the living room where the sound system was blaring loud pop music. She turned it down.

"Friends, I have an announcement to make. Susan here thought it would be funny to show up in her pajamas. I guess she wanted to make us all laugh, so it would be rude not to." Her shrill cries of cruel laughter pierced my ears. My classmates joined in.

"C'mon, Susan, surely you knew this was a hot-tubbing party. Not a pajama party."

She rallied the crowd with her words and soon I was surrounded. The group shuffled me outside to the deck. There were a few people in the large 12-person hot tub. They looked up. Michelle gave them a look and a nod. They took the hint and got out immediately, toweling off, and looking confused.

It didn't take them long to realize what was going on, though.

"Let's get your clothes off, Susan so you can join the party."

The group began clawing at my clothes, pulling them off. Stripping me down to my underwear and bra. I wrapped my arms around myself to preserve some dignity. Before I could do anything, Michelle stepped up, and shoved me hard into the water while she smirked and said, "Don't forget to hold your breath, bitch."

The hot water enveloped me, and I closed my mouth too late. Hot chemical salt water filled my mouth. I broke the surface quickly sputtering and coughing. Hot tears were stinging my eyes. I was thankful that the water hid this fact.

"Did you forget your towel?"

Everyone roared with laughter. My eyes darted around, hoping someone would show a sliver of humanity and compassion. My eyes landed on Maddy. Her expression was pained, but she made no move to help me or stop this cruelty.

It was like a literal punch to the gut. I couldn't restrain the tears. I choked out a sob.

"Are you crying?" Michelle said with glee. "Wittle baby can't handle a hot tub?"

I was defeated. This was too much. I knew that Michelle would be my worst fear and I would not win. I wasn't sure why I even fought so hard with all the other fears. I'd do them all over again if it meant I could simply skip this one.

I was full on ugly crying now, and I didn't care. After all I'd been through and now, I was going to be defeated. It was so unfair.

The laughter roared around me. I continued to cry like a baby.

Then something like quiet resolve nudged at my mind. Wait a minute, I thought. My tears ebbed slightly, and I repeated the thought that had just passed through my mind, but with different inflection.

After everything I'd been through, and I was going to let myself be defeated by this!? This piece of shit! I bested a pedophile for God's sake, and I couldn't take out this scrawny cheerleader? So what she could do back flips.

I suddenly didn't even care that I was half naked. I was seeing red like a flaming neon sign. I climbed out of the tub, and I balled up my fist. I cocked my arm back, and I punched Michelle right in the nose.

Silence fell on the crowd.

Then I heard one guy say, "Damn, she's gonna need a nose job now."

The group began laughing, and I was slow to realize the crowd was now laughing at Michelle.

I was shocked when Maddy came to me with a large beach towel. I reached out tentatively, and when I realized it was a genuine gesture, I grabbed it and wrapped it around myself.

Michelle was doubled over in pain. She scrambled up, sobbing through blood and tears she screamed, "Bitch, I'm going to sue you for this."

"Not before I sue you for instigating fucking assault, you bitch." I screamed after her. Half of my classmates were witnesses to the bullying, and I was pretty sure ripping my clothes off would count as starting shit first.

"Oh, damn." I heard quite a few of them saying.

Maddy was standing in front of me, and she looked pained. I waited for her to say something. Finally, she said, "I'm sorry."

I didn't really know how to respond to that. I had mixed feelings. I had defeated my last fear and my wish would be granted. I suddenly realized with elation. I'd bested my last fear, and my wish was being granted!

I had a moment of exuberance, but it was mixed with something else I couldn't place. I wasn't sure what, but the wish fulfilled didn't seem as gratifying as I'd imagined it would be.

Maddy sighed, "C'mon, let's get you back home and get some dry clothes." She took me by the arm and led me away. The group of students were now breaking up.

As I walked with Maddy, something felt off. My wish had been granted, but this felt wrong. Something was wrong, but I didn't know what.

We made our way across the lawn, to my house. We entered the front door, made our way up the stairs to my room, and as soon as we entered, a harsh whisper floated across the room saying, "You lose. You did not defeat all your fears and the sun will soon rise."

"What no!" I screamed. "I defeated all of them, even Michelle."

The scratchy ethereal whisper repeated itself, "You lose. I will claim you before the hour is up."

"No, you cheated. You fucking cheated! This is bullshit," I screamed. I picked up the book and threw it across the room. It landed on the wall with a thud.

I slumped down on my bed and saw Maddy, frozen like a statue, standing in my room. I'd momentarily forgotten her.

What am I missing? What fear did I not overcome?

I looked outside the window. The world had that gray tint to it, waiting for the first light of dawn to touch down on the world and wake it up.

I had mere minutes to figure this out. C'mon, Susan, figure this out. Think, think.

"You lose," the voice crooned with soft amusement.

"Shut up! I still have time!" I screamed.

I looked up at Maddy, and it hit me. Maddy. The whole reason I'd made the wish in the first place was because I feared being alone. I wanted more than anything for things to go back to the way they were because I hated being alone. She'd always been there, and now she wasn't. I had to make peace with being alone.

I wrapped the towel tightly around my shoulders and stood in front of Maddy. Tears welled up in my eyes as I knew what I needed to do.

"Maddy, we were the best of friends, and I would have done anything for you. I would have gone to hell and back. Fuck, I did go to hell and back. But you abandoned me the first moment that something seemingly better came along. You aren't a real friend. I don't want to be friends with someone who doesn't value me as much as I value them. So, fuck off and go be with your precious Michelle. You deserve each other."

Her body was frozen like a paused frame on a movie screen, but just before I turned away from her, I saw a single tear trickle down her cheek. Then she disappeared.

"Make your wish." The raspy voice whispered grudgingly.

I thought about this, and I didn't know what I wanted. Money, popularity? Maybe. But to be honest, I didn't trust this entity to be forthcoming, so I wished for the one thing that I knew was the safest bet of security.

"I wish for 'The Book of Fear' to go back to whatever realm it was created and leave me alone!"

Just like that the book vanished.

CHAPTER SEVEN

The sun was starting to rise, and I slumped down on the bed. I'd done it. I'd accomplished what hundreds, if not thousands of souls had attempted to do and failed.

It was Sunday, and I knew my parents would be furious, but I crawled under my covers, and I slept all day and night. I didn't wake until Monday morning.

When I got up for school that morning, I was pleasantly surprised that I didn't have any anxiety about going to school. Sure, it had all been an illusion, and I braced myself for the same possibility that I could be Michelle's next target of bullying, but for some reason I knew I could handle it. Even if it meant throwing another crazy haymaker right into her precious porcelain face again.

I no longer pined for Maddy. Now that I'd made peace with the fact that my life had changed and would never go back to the way it was, it gave me a sense of freedom and empowerment, I'd not ever felt before.

I was prepared for whatever the day held, and I felt like I could conquer the world.

As I made my way down the halls, I couldn't help but notice that my classmates would glance at me then whisper to each other.

"What the hell..." I thought to myself.

I rounded the corner, about to enter my first class, one I had to share with both Michelle and Maddy, and they both made eye contact with me.

I was startled to see Michelle's dark bruising across her nose and eyes, and a bandage across the bridge of her nose.

Holy shit!

The realization of what this meant, took me aback. Michelle glared at me then looked away.

Maddy glanced at me for only a second. There was only sadness and regret in her eyes, but I didn't feel sorry for her.

I realized with stunned shock that the events of that night at Michelle's house weren't a mirage, as perhaps the other fears were. It had really happened. And like I said when I began this story, I was never the same after that.

CAN'T GET ENOUGH?

Sign up for The Black Rose
Community Newsletter
and get the FREE 13k word novelette,
"Restricted Section"
sent immediately to your inbox!

The Origin Story!

Why do strange things always happen in Acadia?

SYNOPSIS: Nora knows that her aspirations to be a librarian are quaint and uninspiring, but she doesn't care. She likes knowing what to expect in life. It comes as a great surprise when her friend mentions the 'Restricted Section' hidden in the town library and she becomes downright obsessed to learn more. It's rumored that no soul has visited since a girl died from reading forbidden books, years ago. Now, Nora will stop at nothing to find out what's behind the door of the 'RESTRICTED SECTION!'

IF YOU LOVED THIS BOOK...

Whether you did or didn't, I'd love to know why. I value all feedback as it helps me become a better writer. Leaving a review is a great way to support an indie author like me, so I can continue to publish content more readily for you.

I truly appreciate your taking the time to leave a review on the platform you purchased this from.

It only takes a few minutes of your time, and it helps immensely!

The 'Thank You' story is free regardless, but I'd appreciate that one minute of your time!

Thanks so much in advance!

PREVIEW OF
ANXIETY THERAPY

To Purchase Anxiety Therapy visit:

Books2Read.com/anxiety-therapy

SYNOPSIS:

In the cutthroat world of corporate success, Marilyn, a reigning queen, grapples with near-crippling anxiety that intensifies with each deal brokered. Desperate for relief, she turns to unconventional therapy under Dr. Drye at her unusual clinic.

Despite initial calm in the clinic's serene gardens, Marilyn is soon plunged into the confusion of shadows and nightmares. As the lines blur between reality and horror, she dismisses her intuition, hoping for a cure from her expert doctor. However, when the thin veneer shatters, unveiling a nightmarish reality, Marilyn must confront her own demons or risk being trapped in a prison of terror.

CHAPTER ONE

Memories are a funny, fickle thing. It's like they have a life of their own, and they either own you, or you own them. The lines get blurred on who owns who, the older you get.

There I was, just minding my own business, sitting in my office, typing away at my latest presentation. My eyes drifted to the gift basket that had arrived from one of our clients who had been particularly satisfied with my handling of their accounts.

There was a logo on the bag of coffee beans in the basket that jarred my mind back into my past like a car being t-boned at an intersection. Suddenly, I remembered Adam, a classmate from my middle school years. I hadn't thought about him in decades. That logo on the coffee bag reminded me of this stupid t-shirt he always wore.

Although, it wasn't exactly the memory of his lame t-shirt alone that came hurdling into my mind at mock speed. It was a confrontation between us. The teacher had asked us what we wanted to be when we grew up. Half the classroom's hands shot into the air, including mine. When I was called on, I said I was going to work in New York as a businesswoman.

Before the teacher could even respond, Adam scoffed and said, "Women can't run businesses! That's a man's job!"

It was the early 80s. Looking back, he probably had quintessential 50s parents, where his father taught him "the respective roles of men and women."

I didn't back down, though. I quickly responded, "Shut up. I can be a businesswoman, and I will be. You just watch."

"Whatever," he replied.

Finally, our good-for-nothing teacher interjected, "Now, kids settle down." Then promptly ignored the confrontation between us and moved on to the next student.

I don't know what compelled me to want to succeed so badly in the corporate world. It wasn't until that little memory jogger. Maybe it hinted I had an irrational need to prove myself to a society I felt thought little of me just because I was a woman?

I relished a moment. These moments were far and few between now. I beamed with arrogant pride. *If you could see me now, asshole,* I mumbled to myself. I'd lost track of my old classmate. Never went back to my hometown reunions. Too little time to indulge in ego-driven nostalgia. Which made the consideration about proving myself seem odd.

Maybe I was just born with a rebellious streak. It would explain why I had no trouble shooting off my defenses at Adam. While all my other female friends in high school pined for a fairytale wedding, half a dozen kids, a doting husband, and a cute little house with a picket fence—the All-American dream, I was preoccupied with my own abstract dreams.

I guess the disinterest in the doting husband made sense since I realized some time in my teens I was gay. The rest of the aspirations that ran contrary to the population of female goals and dreams didn't seem normal. I didn't really care, though.

I dreamt of high-rises in New York, sharp, crisp business suits, and the smell of paper and industrial carpet in conference rooms. I know, it almost sounds comical, but it was my fairytale, that I'd made a reality! You have to realize that when I graduated from college in 1994, female corporate executives were about as rare as finding a pink unicorn trotting through Central Park.

I used to hold a great sense of pride in my accomplishments, knowing how rare my accolades were. But now…

Fast forward to 2016, and the realities of the corporate world would soon snuff out my romanticized fantasies of executive success. At least the definition of what I'd come to believe success meant.

To be clear, I achieved every single one of my dreams. I finished college with top marks. I got out of Dodge. I worked my way up to become the CEO of a large corporate firm that dealt with clients from all over the world. I got to travel. I lived in a high-rise penthouse apartment. I had a personal assistant and a chauffeur. When profits were high, sometimes I made more money in a week than most people made in a year.

I never got married, so it goes without saying that I never had kids.

However, there was one relationship that pains me to think about. I came home one day to find her packing her things. I should have been angry, devastated. Looking back, I was, but years of practice at hiding my emotions, made me deter to that behavior.

I watched her cry her eyes out, plead with me. Then I simply let her walk out. Rationalizing that it was the best decision for the both of us.

I realized only after she'd left what a colossal mistake I'd made, letting her go. We often take for granted the peace that runs parallel with having a significant other in your life who would do anything for you. More simply stated, you don't know what you've got until it's gone.

I was so callous, acting like I didn't care. I cared. I just didn't want to admit it to myself. I wouldn't realize until it was years down the road, and too late to do anything about it, how badly my priorities were fucked.

She wanted more time with me. We argued about it a lot. She was simply tired of playing second fiddle to my true love—my career. The success was everything I wanted and more, yet it was also nothing I wanted and probably subconsciously despised. All of it had come at such a heavy price. I was still unwilling to admit how much of the pit I was in had been dug by my own hands.

At first, the success—every deal landed—was an adrenaline rush. I lived for that rush like a drug. But, like all drugs, eventually, the thrill wore off. The proverbial ceiling was hit. It turned into a bargain of anxiety and the avoidance of it.

I developed chronic anxiety and adrenal fatigue. It got worse after Yasmin left me, but I wouldn't let my pride admit that. I could afford the best doctors and cutting-edge medication. They were experts. Why shouldn't they be able to staunch my pain?

For two decades strong, I managed to hide those near-crippling panic attacks. Yet, with every next big deal that needed sealing, anxiety would grip my chest like a vise.

My success rate was over 80%, which was unheard of in my field. Notwithstanding that I was a woman. I knew I had high numbers, *because* I was a woman. I had to work longer and harder than the men, and it paid off. I earned the respect of almost all the men I interacted with, and they never knew how the icy grip of anxiety was slowly tearing me apart from the inside out.

Everything would come to a screeching halt in 2016. You see, the problem with anxiety and medications is that as your anxiety worsens, you have to keep increasing the dose of your little hallowed pills until, eventually, you max it out. And then, you move on to the next latest and greatest little colored tablets your physician prescribes.

I was tired of the monotony, the merry-go-round of ups and downs—doctors and pills. Droning on and on about my tired old story to a therapist who pretended to care. Just so he could garner his paycheck to supplement the facade of a lifestyle where he was prominent and *making a difference* in society. I knew I was a hypocrite for resenting him because I was guilty of the same song and dance.

I guess some part of my soul was searching for different answers. It would happen when I went on a business trip to Hartford, Connecticut, in the spring of 2016.

A woman handed me a neon green flyer as I sat in the coffee shop preparing for the presentation. I took it and set it down. I dismissed the innocuous piece of paper. Ironically, I felt an anxiety attack start to well up. My eyes scrambled to focus on something that would ground me, and they fell upon the flyer.

The paper had copy written on it that was simple and bold saying, *"Do you suffer from anxiety?"* In smaller print, it continued, *"If you are fed up with conventional medication and therapy treatments, try our clinic. We have a 99% success rate of not only treating but curing you of anxiety completely. Call us for your free consultation."*

I scanned the bottom of the flyer, which had the business's name, an address in some town called Acadia, and a phone number. I traveled often to the New England states, and was quite familiar with their bigger cities, and smaller towns. I'd never heard of Acadia. That one managed to elude me.

I also found it slightly odd that there was no email, but then again, many small businesses preferred to do belly-to-belly marketing, so perhaps it wasn't too odd. I resolved I would get through today's presentation and call the number on the flyer immediately after.

The presentation went off without a hitch, and I questioned for the millionth time why I had such panic attacks before these presentations. Tomorrow, we would finalize the paperwork, and all would be well.

Then, late that night, I remembered why I had anxiety. I got an email saying the client had changed their mind and decided to go with our competitor. This was a huge account to land, and I felt the panic setting in.

I was never under the false pretense that my corporate position in life was safe and stable. In my industry, once you got fired, it was almost like getting blacklisted. I dreaded that outcome. And even with a track record of so many successes, I had no illusions that one deal gone wrong would earn you the boot faster than you could blink.

As I paced back and forth, my eyes caught the brilliant green color of the flyer once again. I had laid it on the kitchen counter in my hotel suite. I picked up my phone and dialed the number, thinking to leave a message. It was well past ten p.m. To my surprise, a smooth female voice with a slight accent answered. "Wellness Therapies Complete, this is Dr. Drye. How can I help you?"

I was momentarily speechless. I did not expect an answer at this late hour, much less from the doctor herself. Perhaps this should have been a big red flag. However, when anxiety cripples you and you've already tried everything without much success, you'll do anything to be alleviated from it.

"Hello?" the voice implored.

I stuttered a reply, "Yes, sorry, I just wasn't expecting anyone to answer the line at ten o'clock at night."

"Well, I just happened to be awake." She laughed lightly. "Call me something of a workaholic. And something told me I should answer this call. Doctor's intuition, if you will."

Again, I paused. I could relate to the work habit, but as far as I had experienced, doctors were very dismissive of intuition. This immediately set me on edge, giving me mixed emotions in my first impression of her. Honestly, though, I felt desperate for relief.

"Someone handed me your flyer while I was in Hartford today. It says you do free consultations?"

"Yes, that's correct. First session is free."

"I'm interested in learning more about what your therapies can provide for me."

"Wonderful! I can get you in at 3:00 p.m. tomorrow? My schedule is usually hectic, but you're in luck. I had a cancellation today."

"That would be just fine."

"Great, we'll see you tomorrow, Marilyn."

Then, click, the line went dead.

I stared at the phone, questioning my sanity. I could have sworn that I did not tell Dr. Drye my name. Obviously, I must have. I despised how anxiety could make you feel insane, constantly calling your own mind into question.

The next day, I spent my entire morning pandering to our fickle prospects. Often, clients would use the tactic of saying they were going with the other party, merely to haggle a better price. It was a classic manipulation tactic to land better rates, playing one company off the other to see who would bend to their demands first.

It was my job to determine whether they were serious about dropping us or just playing the game.

After a very harrowing morning and securing the deal, I was exhausted. I was on edge. I was desperate for this new therapy to work for me. As I took an Uber out to Wellness Therapies Complete, in the outlying town of Acadia, I realized I felt an unfamiliar emotion. It had been such a long time since I had hope.

To Purchase Anxiety Therapy visit:

Books2Read.com/anxiety-therapy

About The Black Rose Brands

MARY BLACK ROSE

Studied writing at the "School of Hard Knocks" and "University of Life" getting my degrees in "Fine Arts of Common Sense" with a minor in "Epic Ass-Handing."

Being pansexual, I enjoy writing a variety of LGBTQ characters with diverse backgrounds and sexual orientations. Throw in a dab of magical realism, and romance for good measure, and some real-life conflicts to overcome, and you get 'Black Rose' original stories.

I read a lot to keep the voices in my head quiet. I write a lot to keep the voices alive.

When I'm not writing, I'm supporting my husband and wife, (I'm polyamorous), and taking care of family minions. You might also find me crocheting, hiking, watching Deadpool or South Park yet again, or just reading a good book.

BLACK ROSE READS

Black Rose Reads is my pen name to facilitate writing and narrating speculative paranormal and horror fiction on my YouTube channel @Black Rose Reads, and publishing horror anthologies such as the Twisted Tales Series, and original works of short paranormal horror novelettes in the Eerie Acadia Series.

MISTRESS BLACK ROSE

Here in my imagination, lesbians wield whips and flogs, tie you up and leave you breathless. Naughty subs enjoy a little bondage and spanking.

In my Erotic Lesfic, you will always find happy endings and sweet romance, blended with steamy bondage and submission.

My characters go on a journey, learn valuable lessons, and come full circle, all within the realm of the BDSM Lifestyle.

For FREE stories and more info visit me at:

MaryBlackRose.com – LGBT Magical
   Realism, Speculative Horror, & Cozy Horror

MsBlackRose.com – BDSM & Steamy LGBT
   Romance